MacKenzie Smiles, LLC, San Francisco, CA

www.mackenziesmiles.com

Originally published as *Ruffen. Sjøromen Som Ikke Kunne Svømme*
Copyright © Gyldendal Norsk Forlag AS 1998 [All rights reserved]
www.gyldendal.no
First published by Den Norske Bokkluben 1972

Original text & artwork by Tor Age Bringsvaerd and Thore Hansen

Translation © Copyright James Anderson 2008

Art production by Bernard Prinz

ISBN 978-0-9790347-9-4

Printed in China

10 9 8 7 6 5 4 3 2 1

MACKENZIE
SMILES
San Francisco

Distributed in the U.S. and Canada by:
Ingram Publisher Services
One Ingram Blvd.
P.O. Box 3006
LaVergne, TN 37086
(866) 400-5351

Ruffen

The Sea Serpent Who Couldn't Swim

Tor Age Bringsvaerd
Translated by James Anderson

Illustrated by
Thore Hansen

Far out at sea lies a mysterious island.

It can be seen only on Tuesdays and Fridays.

That's why it isn't on any maps.

On this island is a castle...

...and in this castle lives an old
and eminent family of sea serpents.
So eminent, in fact, that it has a
grandmother who says sea *dragon*
instead of sea *serpent*.

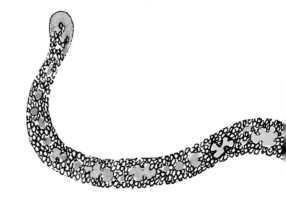

"We must be careful," Grandma says. "If humans discover where we're living, we sea dragons won't ever have a moment's peace."

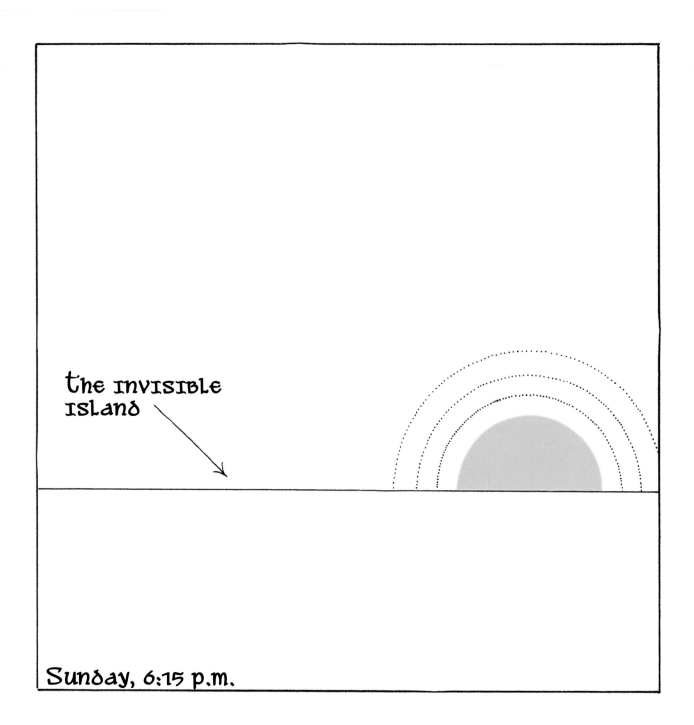

the INVISIBLE
ISLAND

Sunday, 6:15 p.m.

On Sundays, Mondays, Wednesdays, Thursdays, and Saturdays, there's no problem.
The island is invisible, so nobody can find it, no matter how hard people try.
But on Tuesdays and Fridays, things get dangerous.

That's why Uncle Ludwig keeps watch. He lies in a circle right around the island.

Each time a boat or a plane appears, Uncle Ludwig blows hard through his nose. In one big puff, both the island and the castle vanish in thick smoke.

No one knows how Uncle Ludwig does it. *He* doesn't even know.
But it's probably because he's related (distantly and on his mother's side)
to a fire-breathing Chinese dragon. At any rate, everyone agrees that,
without Uncle Ludwig, they would have been discovered long ago.
None of the other sea serpents can puff out so much as a smoke ring,
so Uncle Ludwig is the obvious security guard.

If the night happens to be very chilly, the other
sea serpents take hot cocoa out to Uncle Ludwig.
They're all worried that he might get a cold and
a stuffed-up nose.

It's difficult to say just how many sea serpents
live on the island. Nobody has ever tried to
count them. But there is room for everyone.
The castle has twenty floors above sea level,
and twenty floors below.

A baby sea serpent is only two yards long.

But it quickly gets bigger and it never stops growing.

Long ago, legend has it, there once was a really huge
sea serpent. It was so big that it could stretch around
the world and bite its own tail. But this was rare.
Most sea serpents today are no bigger than a
football field. And some are even smaller.

This tale is about a
very small sea serpent
whose real name was
Arthur – but everyone
called him Ruffen.

Little sea serpents like to play in the water all day long.
They have swimming races on the surface and underwater.
They play hide-and-seek in dark holes and hunt for
treasure in old shipwrecks.

But Ruffen wasn't like the other sea serpents. Ruffen
didn't want to play in the water.

While other sea serpents frolicked about and had fun,
Ruffen sat by himself and watched.

He never went fishing with the others.

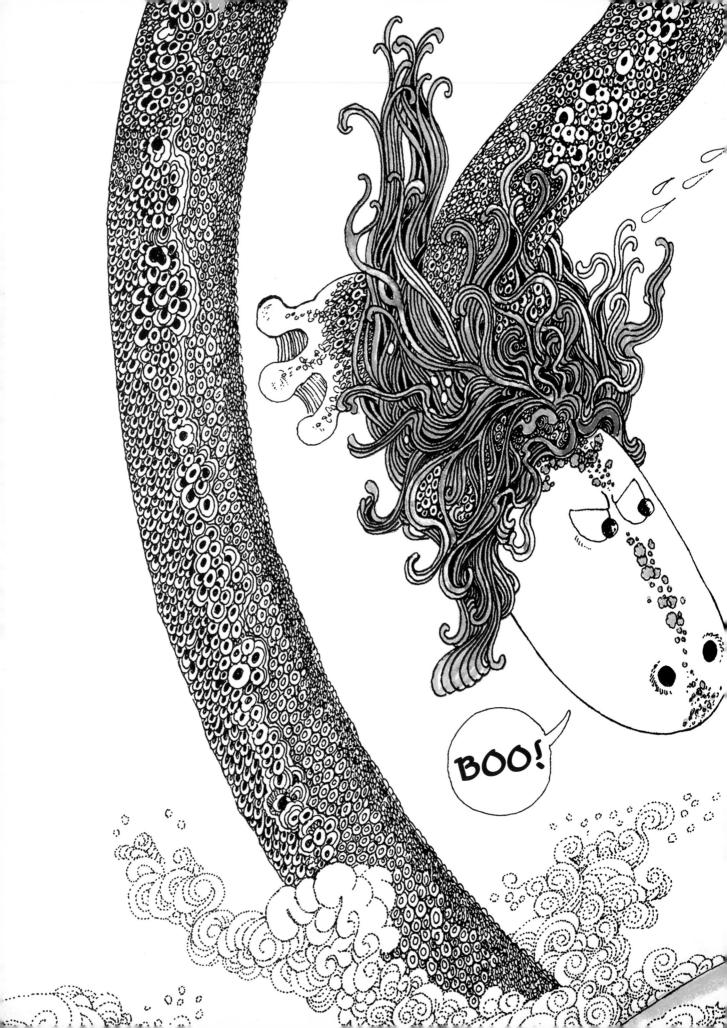

He never joined the other sea
serpents when they popped out of
the waves like jack-in-the-boxes
and shouted, "BOO!" at the big
boats. (For this to work, you have
to frown and look dangerous. If
you giggle nobody will be scared.)

Everyone teased Ruffen.

"Ruffen is afraid to get wet," they called out. "Ruffen is scared of the water." And they splashed him.

Then Ruffen would run off and hide deep inside the castle. Sometimes he cried, but only when nobody could see him.

"What in the seven seas are we going to do about Ruffen?" the grown-ups wondered. "He's a disgrace to the entire family. Whoever heard of a sea serpent who is scared of the water?"

"Don't worry," said Grandma. "He's sure to grow out of it. Ruffen will become a fine sea dragon. I can feel it in my tail."

One day, while Ruffen was crawling around
by himself picking flowers, he heard someone
moaning down by the water's edge.
"Bother and drat it," the voice exclaimed.
"Double bother and drat it a dozen times."

A large octopus had caught one of its tentacles between two rocks and couldn't get free again.

"How in the world of waves did that happen?" Ruffen asked in amazement.

The octopus blushed. "I'm a real terror for swimming in my sleep," he said with embarrassment. "Sometimes I wake up miles away from my bed. But this is the first time I've gotten trapped."

"Let me help you," said Ruffen.

He used his tail as a crowbar and rolled the rocks away. The octopus sighed with relief.

"Thank you," he said happily. "It's wonderful to be able to use all eight arms again."

Then he bowed to Ruffen. "My name is Fourteen Ninety-Two," he announced.

"Fourteen Ninety-Two!" said Ruffen.
"You can't be called that. Fourteen Ninety-Two isn't a name, it's a number."

"Of course it's a number," said Fourteen Ninety-Two. "And a very fine number it is. I'm actually named after Christopher Columbus' first voyage to the Americas."

Ruffen had no idea who Christopher Columbus was, but he thought it would be silly to ask. So he nodded wisely and pretended to understand. "But perhaps you've got another name as well?" he asked cautiously.

"Naturally," said the octopus. "Fourteen Ninety-Two is only my first number. I've got a second number, too."

"You mean first name and second name," said Ruffen.

"If I'd meant that, I'd have said it," replied Fourteen Ninety-Two.

"And what is your second name...I mean, your second number?"

"Point Two Five," said Fourteen Ninety-Two earnestly. "So my real name is 1492.25. But everyone just calls me Fourteen Ninety-Two."

"My name is Ruffen," said Ruffen. Suddenly, it sounded very ordinary, almost as if he didn't have a name at all.

"Tell me more about what it's like to swim in your sleep," begged Ruffen.

"It's not much fun, if that's what you think," said Fourteen Ninety-Two. "In fact, it's extremely annoying." He waved his arms in despair. "I've tried tying myself down, but it's impossible to sleep with a rope around my tummy."

"But what about me, then?" said Ruffen sadly. "I can't swim at all!"

Fourteen Ninety-Two gawked. "You can't swim?"

Without waiting for a reply, he disappeared among the waves and sank to the ocean floor. (This is what octopuses do when something really amazes them.)

When Fourteen Ninety-Two surfaced again, he was in a serious mood. "Don't you like to swim?" he asked.

Ruffen looked down. "I was sick the summer the other little sea serpents learned to swim," he said.

Fourteen Ninety-Two nodded. "And since then you've found it embarrassing swimming with them?"

"All the others can swim," Ruffen sighed. "They just tease me and splash water at me. They say they'll give me a dunking."

Fourteen Ninety-Two folded his arms into a big, determined knot. "I'm really on vacation and heading for the Canary Islands," he said. "But one good deed deserves another. I'll teach you to swim. I'm not leaving here until you're swimming like a speedboat!"

And that was how Ruffen made a friend.

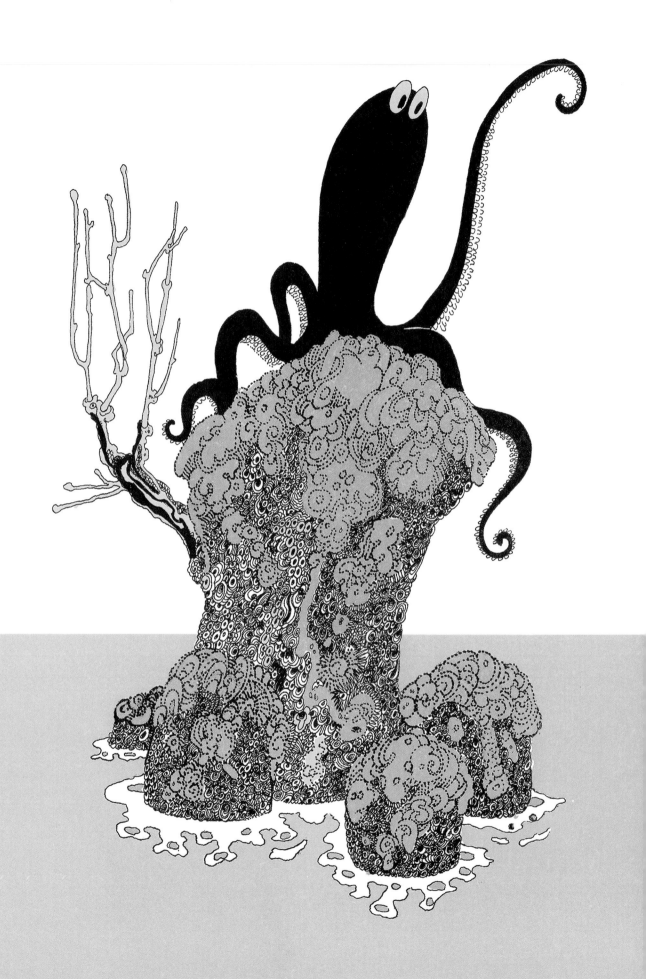

They began training right away.

"First of all, you must get used to getting water on your face," said Fourteen Ninety-Two.

Ruffen waded cautiously around in the shallows and splashed himself with water.

Then he had to put his head underwater.

"Keep your eyes open!" shouted Fourteen Ninety-Two.

It didn't hurt at all.

Ruffen thought everything underwater looked so beautiful that he didn't want to stop looking at it.

The two friends trained every day. Learning to swim was fun now, Ruffen thought, because nobody was teasing him or being nasty. But he made very sure that the other sea serpents wouldn't find out about his swimming lessons. Just wait, he thought. One day I'll surprise them all.

To begin with, Fourteen Ninety-Two held two
of his arms under Ruffen's belly. Soon Ruffen
was able to swim several strokes on his own.
And he quickly got better.

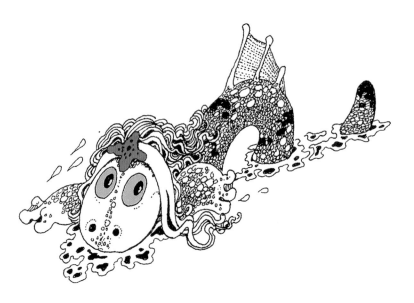

He learned to swim on his back.

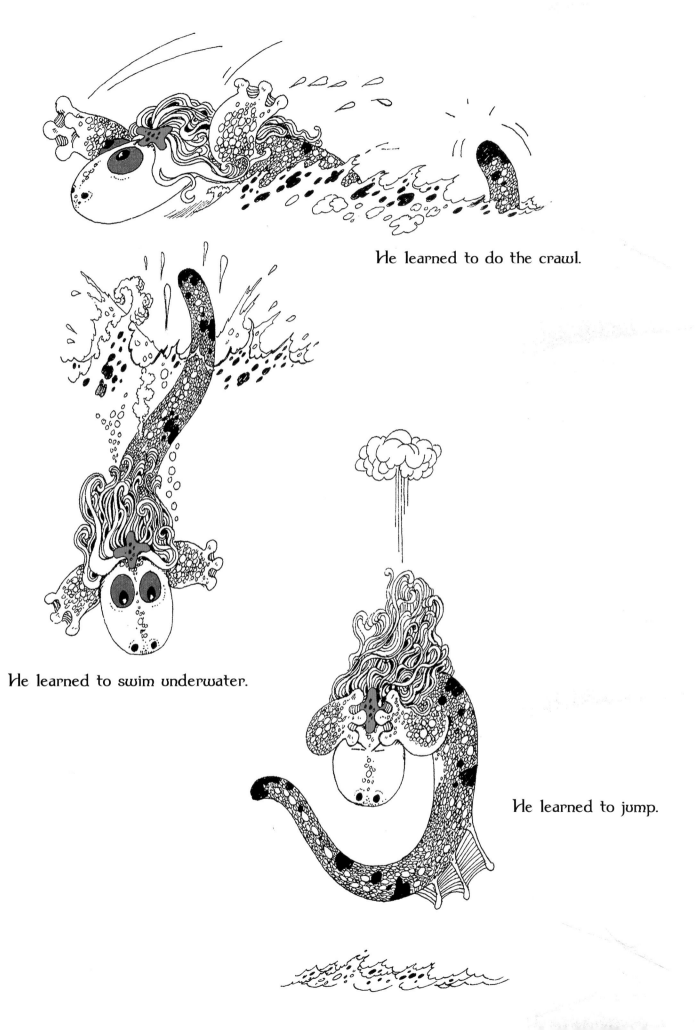

He learned to do the crawl.

He learned to swim underwater.

He learned to jump.

He learned to dive.

Then one day Fourteen Ninety-Two said, "There's nothing more I can teach you, Ruffen. You can swim as well as me now. Maybe even better."

The two friends said good-bye to each other. Ruffen stayed behind. And Fourteen Ninety-Two was able to swim south at last toward the Canary Islands.

"Have a nice vacation," Ruffen called after him.

That night there was a terrible storm. It was the worst storm in serpent memory. Even Grandma couldn't recall anything like it. Poor Uncle Ludwig was almost blown away. There was so much thunder and lightning that nobody dared to sleep. All the sea serpents huddled together looking out the windows.

"I pity anyone who's out at sea tonight," said
Grandma, as she sat there tut-tutting with her head
in crabs. (Sea serpents use crabs as hair clips.)

All of a sudden they caught sight of a red rocket hissing through the sky. And then another one!

A big ocean liner was sinking and it was firing rockets to ask for help.

"We must do something!" said Grandma.

"Yes," said all the sea serpents. "We must do something."

But nobody did anything.

Aboard the ocean liner, all the passengers were rushing around the decks shouting for help. Many of them hadn't even managed to get dressed properly. They ran about in pajamas and nightgowns. A worried-looking brass band played old marches because that often helps when there's an emergency at sea.

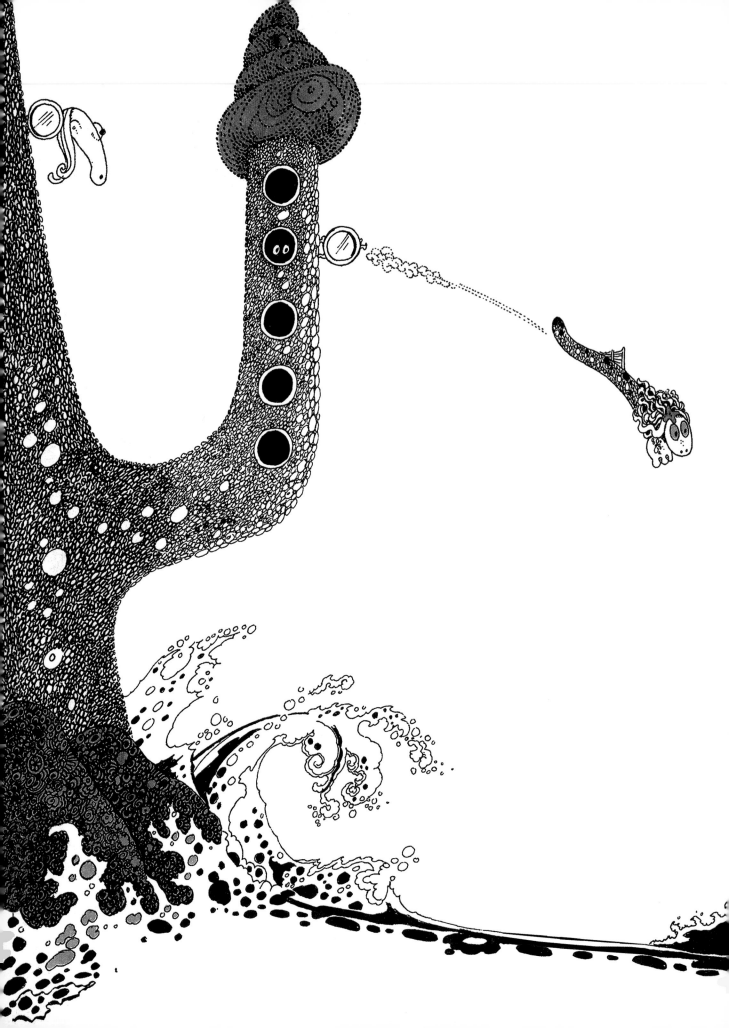

"We must swim out and save them," Grandma insisted.

"Yes," answered the sea serpents. "We must swim out and save them."

But nobody dared to swim into the dangerous hurricane. Even though the sea serpents were on the twentieth floor, the waves still managed to reach right up to the windows.

Suddenly someone opened a window and dove out!

It was Ruffen!

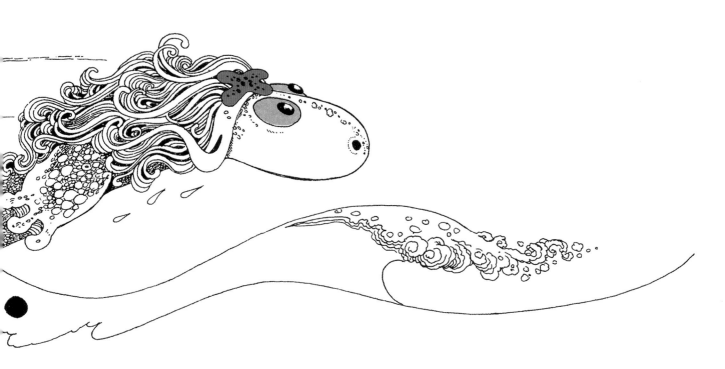

"But he can't even swim!" shouted the other
sea serpents. "He'll get killed. Poor Ruffen,
he's obviously gone totally crazy."

But Ruffen did the crawl up and down the
waves at top speed. He held a steady course
as his tail worked like a propeller.

When the brass band caught sight of Ruffen, they forgot to play, and a couple of the trumpet players fainted.

The captain bit his nails so hard he almost chewed up his whole hand. "Oh, no! Oh, no!" he wailed. "Having a ship about to sink is bad enough. Now we're being attacked by a terrible sea serpent. Anything can happen tonight!"

The passengers screamed and ran in all directions when Ruffen raised his head out of the water and rested his chin on the deck.

"Don't be scared. I've come to help you!" shouted Ruffen. But either the wind was too strong, or nobody understood what he was saying. Many human beings don't understand what animals say.

Ruffen put the anchor chain in his mouth and
pulled the big ocean liner behind him.

All night long, through storm and waves,
he towed the big ship behind him.

The storm didn't die out until the next morning. Then the sea calmed down, and the bad weather swirled behind them like a great spinning top on the horizon.

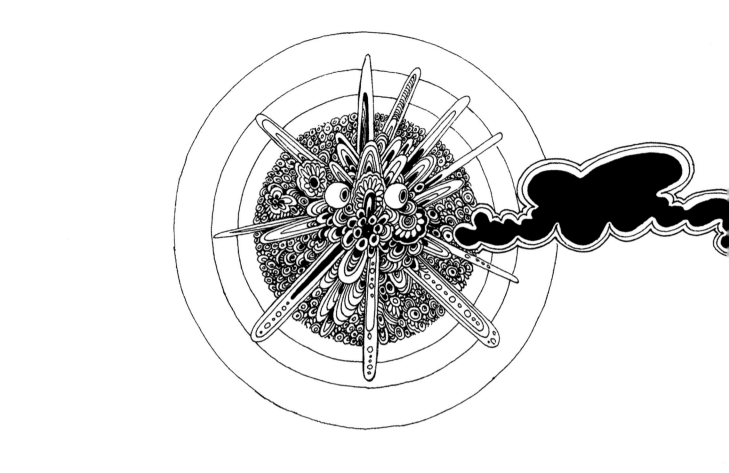
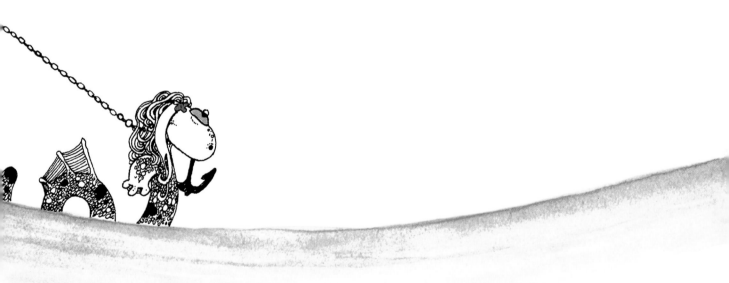

It was only then that the passengers
realized Ruffen had saved them, and that
he wasn't a dangerous monster.

But Ruffen pretended not to notice.

He just kept swimming on and on.

And he didn't stop until he reached America.

There was great jubilation when Ruffen came swimming into New York Harbor. Many people thought the big ocean liner had been lost. No one expected it to be on time after such a huge storm.

Ruffen was the hero of the hour and was presented with a huge gold medal. Everyone gave him three cheers. The mayor made a speech on television and a large girls' choir sang every national anthem in the world from the top of the United Nations building.

Ruffen didn't stay long in New York. He held on to the pier until he got his breath back. Then he pushed off and swam away.

He kept his head high above the water because he was afraid of getting the gold medal round his neck wet.

He thought of what the other sea serpents would say when he got home. And he was so happy that he sang his favorite song all the way home.

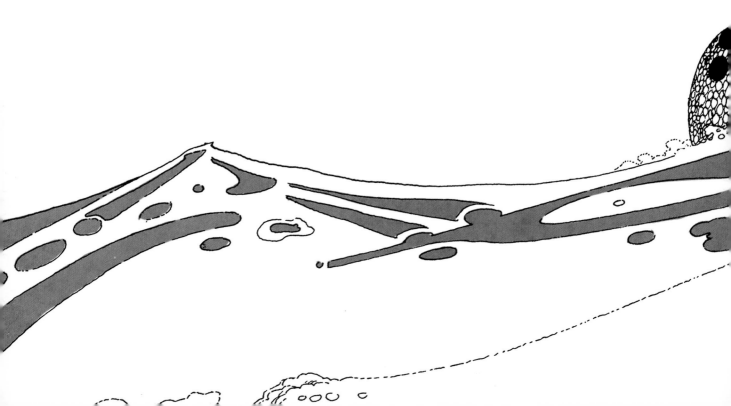

RUFFEN'S SONG

Once there was a dragon
who flew and spouted fire.
His tummy was all hairy
and his head like bristly wire.
His teeth were sharp,
his claws were long,
his manner fierce and bold.
Yet everyone who knew him said
he had a heart of gold.

His name was
Rudolf Jonathon Carl Frederick the Grand.
His wings were weak
so he flew with help
from a twisted rubber band.
And when the other dragons
saw him fly above the land,
their voices raised to shout the praise of
Frederick the Grand.

Ruffen's Song